DRIVE THRU

FUSION

THE COURSE TO
CHOCOLATE

by Harriet Brundle

The Chocolate Box

BEARPORT
PUBLISHING

Minneapolis, Minnesota

Credits

All images are courtesy of Shutterstock.com, unless otherwise specified.
With thanks to Getty Images, Thinkstock Photo, and iStockphoto.

Cover images - kondratya, DKDesignz, surabhi25, Cute little things, Valentyn Volkov, wasapohn.
Recurring images - kondratya, DKDesignz, urabhi25, Cute little things, Valentyn Volkov, Walnut Bird, Mark Olivier, wasapohn, NotionPic. 6 - Hans Geel. 7 - nnattalli. 8 - Kaiskynet Studio. 9 - noBorders - Brayden Howie. 10 - mavo. 11 - Narong Khueankaew. 12 - CHUNG.PT. 13 - photowind. 14 - fjmolina. 15 - grafvision. 16 - wavebreakmedia. 17 - industryviews. 18 - Jozef Sowa. 18&19 - Africa Studio. 19 - Aleksandrova Karina, Pixel-Shot. 20 - ninikas , EQRoy, jabiru, Pavlo Lys, Sergey Lapin. 21 - LightField Studios, Motortion Films, Natasha Breen, StockImageFactory.com.

Library of Congress Cataloging-in-Publication Data

Names: Brundle, Harriet, author.
Title: The course to chocolate / by Harriet Brundle.
Description: Fusion books. | Minneapolis, MN : Bearport Publishing Company, [2022] | Series: Drive thru | Includes bibliographical references and index.
Identifiers: LCCN 2021011425 (print) | LCCN 2021011426 (ebook) | ISBN 9781647479459 (library binding) | ISBN 9781647479534 (paperback) | ISBN 9781647479619 (ebook)
Subjects: LCSH: Chocolate processing--Juvenile literature. | Chocolate--Juvenile literature.
Classification: LCC TP640 .B 2022 (print) | LCC TP640 (ebook) | DDC 664/.5--dc23
LC record available at https://lccn.loc.gov/2021011425
LC ebook record available at https://lccn.loc.gov/2021011426

© 2022 Booklife Publishing
This edition is published by arrangement with Booklife Publishing.

North American adaptations © 2022 Bearport Publishing Company. All rights reserved. No part of this publication may be reproduced in whole or in part, stored in any retrieval system, or transmitted in any form or by any means, electronic, mechanical, photocopying, recording, or otherwise, without written permission from the publisher.

For more information, write to Bearport Publishing, 5357 Penn Avenue South, Minneapolis, MN 55419. Printed in the United States of America.

CONTENTS

Hop in the Chocolate Box...... 4

The Course to Chocolate 6

Inside the Pod................ 8

At the Factory............... 10

Grind It Up 12

In the Mix 14

Taking Shape 16

Sweet Chocolate 18

All the Flavors 20

Chocolate Time!............. 22

Glossary 24

Index 24

HOP IN THE CHOCOLATE BOX

Hello! My name is Kwame and this is my food truck, the Chocolate Box. Which of my tasty chocolate bars would you like to try?

* MENU *

Milk chocolate

Dark chocolate

White chocolate

Chocolate caramel

Oh no! I've run out of chocolate! I need to go get some more. Hop in the Chocolate Box and come with me!

The Chocolate Box

THE COURSE TO CHOCOLATE

Chocolate is made from cocoa beans. The beans come from cacao trees.

Cocoa beans

Cocoa pods growing on a cacao tree

Cacao trees grow pods that have cocoa beans inside. To get the beans, people cut the pods from the trees.

INSIDE THE POD

Then, the pods are cut open. Cocoa beans and white **pulp** are taken out and are left to **ferment**.

Cocoa beans covered in pulp

After fermenting, the beans are dried. Sometimes, they are dried by machines. Other times, they are dried under the hot sun.

AT THE FACTORY

Next, the dried beans go to a factory, where they are cleaned and **roasted**. Roasting brings out the chocolate flavor.

After roasting, the beans' shells are taken away. Only cocoa nibs are left.

Cocoa nibs

GRIND IT UP

The nibs are **ground** up. This makes a very thick, dark **liquid** called cocoa mass.

12

The cocoa mass is made up of cocoa butter and cocoa **solids**. Cocoa butter is the fatty part of chocolate. Cocoa solids are dry and give the chocolate flavor.

13

IN THE MIX

Other **ingredients** are mixed into the cocoa mass to make chocolate. The mixture is put into a machine that stirs it to make it smooth.

Next, the chocolate is heated and cooled. This makes it shiny.

Chocolate is often cooled by a machine. But some people do it by hand.

TAKING SHAPE

The liquid chocolate is then shaped. Chocolate can be made into bars, hearts, stars, and more.

The chocolates cool down until they become hard. Then, they are ready to be eaten!

SWEET CHOCOLATE

Different kinds of chocolate have different ingredients mixed in.

Milk chocolate is often made using cocoa solids, cocoa butter, sugar, and milk.

MILK CHOCOLATE

White chocolate usually has cocoa butter, sugar, and milk. There are no cocoa solids.

WHITE CHOCOLATE

Dark chocolate often has cocoa solids, cocoa butter, and sugar. It skips the milk.

DARK CHOCOLATE

ALL THE FLAVORS

Some chocolate bars also have wafers, caramel, or **nougat**.

WAFERS

CARAMEL

NOUGAT

Lots of things can be added to chocolate. Nuts and fruit are popular choices. What's your favorite kind of chocolate?

Some people even enjoy chili pepper chocolate!

21

CHOCOLATE TIME!

I hope you enjoyed our trip! We've made it back with plenty of chocolate. What would you like to eat?

The Chocolate Box

* MENU *

Milk chocolate

Dark chocolate

White chocolate

Chocolate caramel

Chocolate is tasty, but eating too much of it is not healthy. Enjoy chocolate only as a special treat!

GLOSSARY

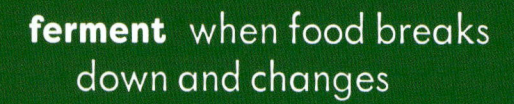

ferment when food breaks down and changes

ground broken into very tiny pieces

ingredients different things that are used to make food

liquid a thing that flows and has no set shape, such as water

nougat a sugary food that usually contains nuts or pieces of fruit

pulp the inner, juicy part of a fruit or vegetable

roasted cooked in a way that gets very hot and dry

solids things that hold their shape and are firm

INDEX

beans 6–11
cocoa butter 13, 18–19
cocoa solids 13, 18–19
ferment 8–9
flavor 10, 13, 20
nibs 11–12
pods 7–8
pulp 8